This book
belongs to:

Just imagine . . . growing, **flying**, sleep
blowing, **swimming**, eating, playing,
rollerskating, parent-frightening, **readi**
falling, **bird-riding**, washing, sailing, le
rusting, unravelling, **nibbling**, scarin
dinosaur-hunting, chariot-riding, chimn
demonstrating, fancy-dressing, **jousting**,
rumbling, **rolling**, grinding, clanging, pu
squeaking, huffing, **bubbling**, spell-ca
charming, rope-climbing, magic-carpet
brewing, **Pegasus-riding**, roaring, **howli**
chomping, leaping, **chewing**, splashing
buzzing, **snorting**, bounding, resting, tr
scuttling, scurrying, **jumping**, walking
tunnelling, digging, fossil-hunting, **burro**
cycling, wheeling, **driving**, unicycling, mc
riding, **helicopter-flying**, diving, floatin

, sneezing, walking, **shouting**, chasing,
scuing, **shrinking**, writing, climbing,
running, biting, drinking, **escaping**,
ning, transforming, **wobbling**, melting,
stretching, popping, time-travelling,
sweeping, **spaceship-flying**, evacuating,
ng, Viking-meeting, **inventing**, whirring,
ng, buzzing, **creaking**, slurping, beeping,
ng, wish-granting, bewitching, **snake-**
ling, **fire-breathing**, egg-laying, potion-
, changing, hanging, racing, **crawling**,
swinging, **sliding**, slithering, laughing,
ing, munching, nibbling, **ball-chasing**,
eeding, cuddling, creeping, **exploring**,
ng, painting, treasure-hunting, **whizzing**,
rbiking, **hang-gliding**, hot-air ballooning,
gliding, sinking, discovering, **dreaming**.

For everyone who loves Heffers Children's Bookshop
– P.G.

For Lily, Lucy, Emily, Jessica, Florence and Henry
– N.S.

PUFFIN BOOKS

UK | USA | Canada | Ireland | Australia
India | New Zealand | South Africa

Puffin Books is part of the Penguin Random House group of companies
whose addresses can be found at global.penguinrandomhouse.com.

www.penguin.co.uk   www.puffin.co.uk   www.ladybird.co.uk

Penguin
Random House
UK

Doubleday edition published 2012
Picture Corgi edition published 2013
This edition published 2022

002

Text copyright © Pippa Goodhart 2012
Illustrations copyright © Nick Sharratt 2012
The moral right of the author and illustrator has been asserted

Printed in China

The authorized representative in the EEA is Penguin Random House Ireland,
Morrison Chambers, 32 Nassau Street, Dublin D02 YH68

A CIP catalogue record for this book is available from the British Library

ISBN: 978–0–241–61990–2

All correspondence to:
Puffin Books, Penguin Random House Children's
One Embassy Gardens, 8 Viaduct Gardens, London SW11 7BW

MIX
Paper from
responsible sources
FSC
www.fsc.org   FSC® C018179

JUST IMAGINE

Imagine being as big as a house!

Or as tiny as a flea!

Take a look inside this book, and decide what you'd like to be.

Nick Sharratt & Pippa Goodhart

PUFFIN

Can you imagine being BIG?

Or would you like to be small?

Imagine being made differently

– not really human at all.

Would you like

to travel through time?

Imagine being magical

Imagine being an animal,

living in the wild.

Perhaps you'd rather be a pet, belonging to some child.

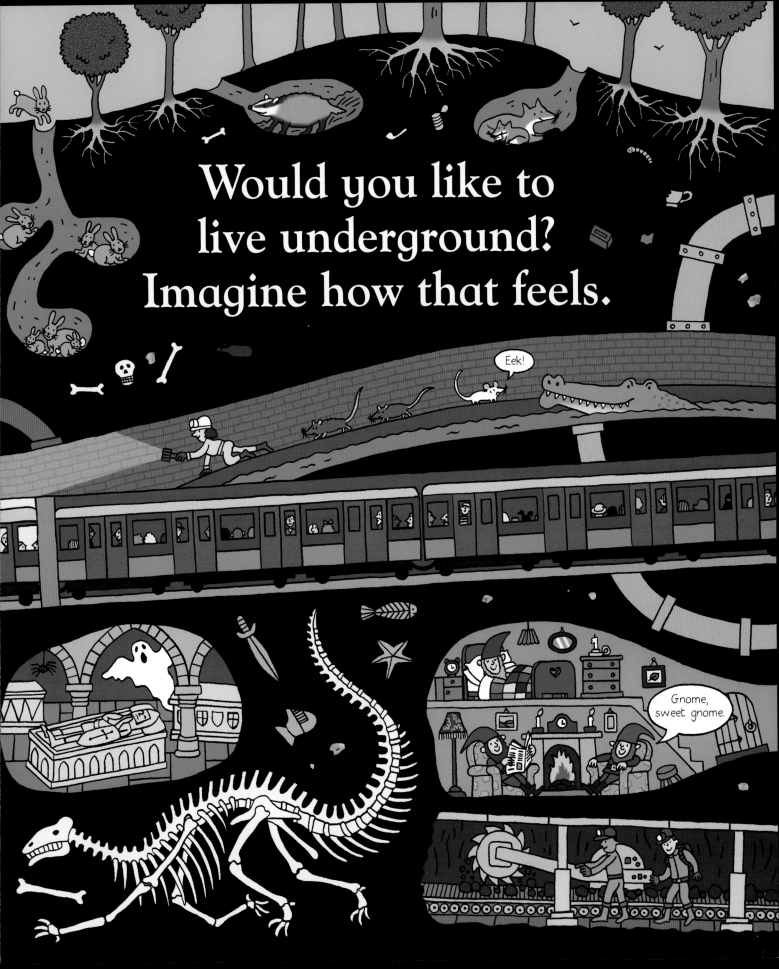

Or would you
like to whizz around
on some kind of wheels?

or living in the sea.

Close your eyes and dream yourself

Just imagine . . . growing, **flying**, sleep
blowing, **swimming**, eating, playing,
rollerskating, parent-frightening, **readi**
falling, **bird-riding**, washing, sailing, le
rusting, unravelling, **nibbling**, scarin
dinosaur-hunting, chariot-riding, chimne
demonstrating, fancy-dressing, **jousting**,
rumbling, **rolling**, grinding, clanging, pu
squeaking, huffing, **bubbling**, spell-ca
charming, rope-climbing, magic-carpet
brewing, **Pegasus-riding**, roaring, **howli**
chomping, leaping, **chewing**, splashing
buzzing, **snorting**, bounding, resting, tr
scuttling, scurrying, **jumping**, walking
tunnelling, digging, fossil-hunting, **burro**
cycling, wheeling, **driving**, unicycling, mc
riding, **helicopter-flying**, diving, floatin

, sneezing, walking, **shouting**, chasing,
scuing, **shrinking**, writing, climbing,
running, biting, drinking, **escaping**,
ning, transforming, **wobbling**, melting,
stretching, popping, time-travelling,
sweeping, **spaceship-flying**, evacuating,
ng, Viking-meeting, **inventing**, whirring,
ng, buzzing, **creaking**, slurping, beeping,
ng, wish-granting, bewitching, **snake-**
ling, **fire-breathing**, egg-laying, potion-
, changing, hanging, racing, **crawling**,
swinging, **sliding**, slithering, laughing,
ing, munching, nibbling, **ball-chasing**,
eeding, cuddling, creeping, **exploring**,
ng, painting, treasure-hunting, **whizzing**,
rbiking, **hang-gliding**, hot-air ballooning,
gliding, sinking, discovering, **dreaming**.

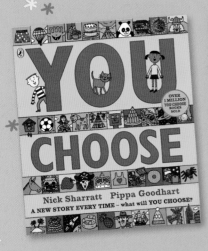

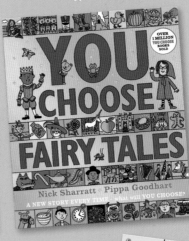

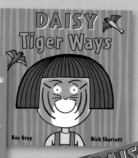

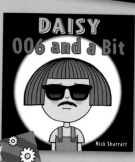

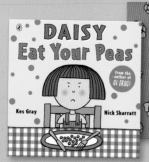

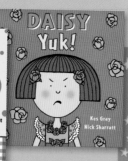

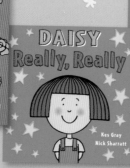

Why not choose
some more books
illustrated by Nick Sharratt?